LITTLE BOAT

Michel Gay

EAU CLAIRE DISTRICT LIBRARY
Macmillan Publishing Company
New York

© 1983, l'école des loisirs, Paris
Translation Copyright © 1985 Macmillan Publishing Company, a division of Macmillan, Inc. All rights reserved.
Library of Congress Cataloging in Publication Data
appears on the last page of this book.

T 111823

I'm going fishing.

I toot my whistle
to say good-by.

I send up
clouds of smoke,

and you can see me
from far away.

I catch lots of fish.

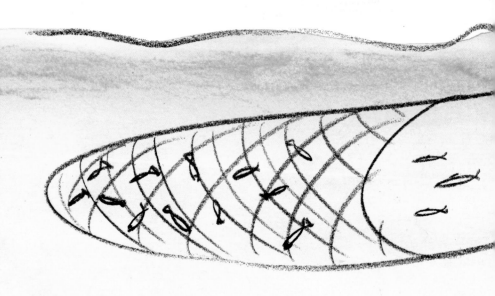

It's hard,
because the waves

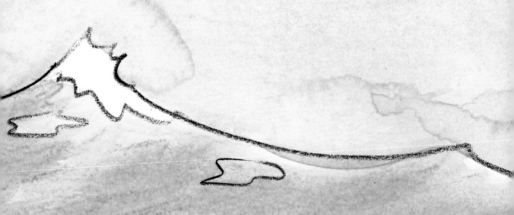

are getting bigger and bigger.

What a storm!
I swallow salt water.

I can't see anything.
It's already night.

There's some light over there....

It's the lighthouse!

It shows me
the way

home to port.

Library of Congress Cataloging in Publication Data
Cox, Michael.
Little boat.
Translation of: Petit bateau.
Summary: A little boat goes out fishing and runs into
a storm.
1. Children's stories, French. [1. Boats and
Boating—Fiction] I. Title
PZ7.G238Lg 1986   [E]   86-42985
ISBN 0-02-737550-1
ISBN 0-02-737540-4 (lib. bdg.)